When I eat

Copyright © 1991 Firefly Books Ltd., Hove, East Sussex.
First published 1991 Firefly Books Ltd.

Library of Congress Cataloging-in-Publication Data

Suhr, Mandy.
    When I eat / by Mandy Suhr; illustrated by Mike Gordon.
        p.   cm. – (I'm alive)
    Summary: A simple explanation of how people, animals, and plants eat and make use of their food.
    ISBN 0-87614-737-6 (lib. bdg.)
    1. Nutrition–Juvenile literature. [1. Food. 2. Digestion. 3. Nutrition.] I. Gordon, Mike, ill. II. Title. III. Series: Suhr, Mandy. I'm alive.
QP141.S837 1992
574.1′3–dc20   91-36755
                                                      CIP
                                                        AC

Printed in Belgium by Casterman, S.A.
Bound in the United States of America

1 2 3 4 5 6 7 8 9 10 01 00 99 98 97 96 95 94 93 92

When I eat

written by Mandy Suhr
illustrated by Mike Gordon

I'm alive!

Carolrhoda Books, Inc./Minneapolis

When I was a tiny baby,
I had no teeth.
I couldn't chew,
but I could suck,
so I drank
lots of milk.

4

Milk is good for many other
kinds of babies too.

As I grew older, I could eat soft, squashy baby food.

Then my teeth started to grow.

8

Soon I had strong teeth, and I could eat all sorts of food. I need food to give my body energy to move and grow.

When I put food into my mouth,
I chew it up and swallow it.

Then the food begins its journey
through my body. The food
travels down my throat
and through a long tube
into my stomach.

Rumble
Rumble

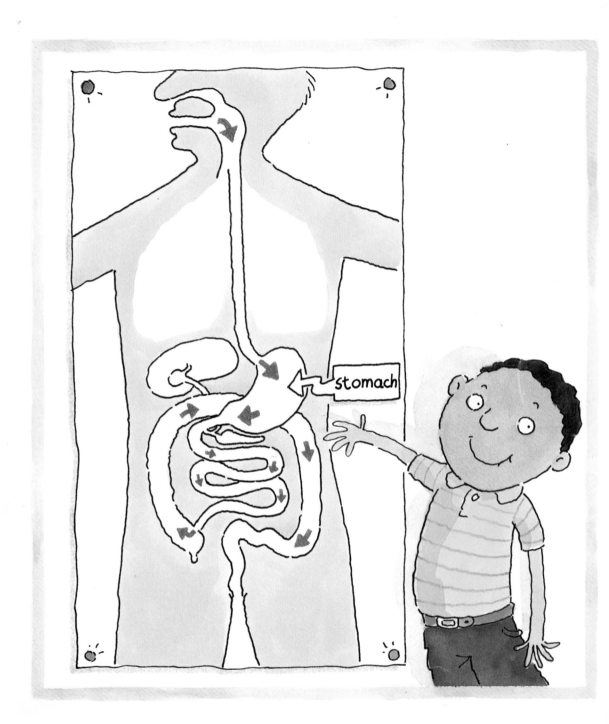

stomach

In my stomach, my body begins to break the food into tiny pieces. These pieces go into a long, curly tube. This tube sorts the parts of food I need from the parts I don't need.

The parts of food I need are sent right into my blood.

And my blood carries these useful parts around my body to where they are needed.

My body gets rid of the food it doesn't use…

when I go to the toilet.

My pets need food just as I do.
I feed them food that is just right
for them.

Animals in the wild find their own
food. Some find plants that are good
for them, and some catch other
animals to eat.

Plants use energy
from the sun to
make their
own food.
This food is
made and
stored in
their leaves.

Plants also suck up minerals from
the soil through their roots.
These minerals help them grow.

Some foods are better
for me than others. Good
foods are full of the things
that make my body
work properly.

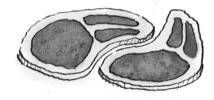

Milk and cheese,
meat, fish, and beans
have proteins that
help me grow.

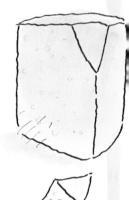

Fruits and vegetables have vitamins and minerals that help me stay healthy.

Bread, potatoes, and pasta give me energy.

I should eat lots of these good foods to grow strong and healthy.

These are some of my favorite things to eat. What are some of your favorite foods?

A note to adults

"I'm Alive" is a series of books designed especially for preschoolers and beginning readers. These books look at how the human body works and develops. They compare the human body to plants and animals that are already familiar to children.

Here are some activities that use what kids already know to learn more about what happens when we eat.

Activities

1. To stay healthy, we need to eat different kinds of foods. Draw pictures of what you eat in one day. Do you eat foods that are good for you?

2. Lots of things we eat are really a mixture of foods. Next time someone is cooking at your house, spend some time in the kitchen watching or helping. Talk to an adult about what the food you eat is made from. Can you figure out how many different foods are in a sandwich? How about in a pizza? Or a chocolate chip cookie?

3. What do you think kids in other countries eat? Ask your teacher or your family to help you find out. Do you know someone from another country? What is his or her favorite food?

4. Not everyone has enough to eat. People who don't have much money may go hungry. Talk to your family or teacher about what you can do to help.

24